MAGIC COMES
IN ITS TIME

Oct. 1993

To Danielle & Joel,

I wish you all the
magic that life can bring!

Doron,
[signature]

MAGIC COMES IN ITS TIME

BERNIECE RABE
ILLUSTRATED BY DORON BEN-AMI

SIMON & SCHUSTER BOOKS FOR YOUNG READERS
Published by Simon & Schuster
New York   London   Toronto   Sydney   Tokyo   Singapore

SIMON & SCHUSTER BOOKS FOR YOUNG READERS
Simon & Schuster Building, Rockefeller Center
1230 Avenue of the Americas, New York, New York 10020
Text copyright © 1993 by Berniece Rabe
Illustrations copyright © 1993 by Doron Ben-Ami
SIMON & SCHUSTER BOOKS FOR YOUNG READERS
is a trademark of Simon & Schuster.
Designed by Vicki Kalajian.
The text of this book is set in ITC Garamond Light.
Manufactured in the United States of America

10   9   8   7   6   5   4   3   2   1

Library of Congress Cataloging-in-Publication Data
Rabe, Berniece.
Magic comes in its time / by Berniece Rabe ;
illustrated by Doron Ben-Ami.   p.   cm.
Summary: Jonathan, an adopted child with no siblings,
hopes that the arrival of storks to his German neighborhood
will signal the arrival of a new baby brother.
[1. Storks—Fiction.   2. Adoption—Fiction.
3. Babies—Fiction.   4. Germany—Fiction.]
I. Ben-Ami, Doron, ill.   II. Title.
PZ7.R105Mag   1993   [Fic]—dc20   92–19260   CIP
ISBN: 0–671–79454–x

To Collin Rabe,
who makes magic happen

CHAPTER ONE

I t was the storks' arrival that had brought Jonathan the best luck ever. Because of their magic, an American army doctor and his wife had adopted him at birth. When Jonathan was not quite three, the storks brought good luck a second time. The same day the storks left Germany for Africa, Jonathan's father was transferred back to the United States. That time stork-luck brought a long, long stay in Atlanta.

Now Dad said that they were to return to Germany and that Jonathan would like it. Mother agreed, reminding him of the storks. But no matter what Dad or Mother said, Jonathan didn't think he'd ever like Germany. Atlanta was his home. The place where his friends were.

However, remembering the magic of the storks, Jonathan squared his shoulders and held his head high. Their magic would get him through. He'd not tell his parents how he felt. Army kids have to be willing to move at any time. It wasn't Dad's fault. The army just needed another doctor in Germany.

Dad had said, "You'll have fun making new friends. A talker like you will have no trouble." Then he'd ruffled up Jonathan's hair and added lovingly, "Hey, travel can broaden a boy's horizons." Whatever that meant.

Mother had said, "You'll love getting in touch with your roots." Jonathan knew that meant he'd be seeing his birthplace.

She'd added, "I know how you love the storks. You deserve to see them."

She was right about that. He always loved her story of how the storks had brought him. He let her go on with her happy talk.

"We'll have just enough time to get settled in before the storks come. Then we'll be free to enjoy them more. Later, we'll have fun traveling to places. You'll love the villages and seeing real castles. But, of course, the first thing, Jonathan, is that you must start school."

Jonathan wanted the storks to come before he started school. He needed their luck to face a new school in a strange land, far from friends.

He pretended they weren't moving until one day Dad sold their car. He would buy a new one in Germany, he said. The next day the army movers came in, packed, and hauled away all their belongings. They slept in a hotel that night, and the next day they flew to Germany. It was shocking. He thought hard about seeing the storks and tried not to think of friends he'd told good-bye.

In Germany, driving along in their new car, Mother and Dad kept pointing out the beauty of the land. Jonathan hardly saw the rolling hills and quaint little towns. His thoughts were on school, among strangers. Two days later Jonathan started off for his new school alone, no sign of a stork in sight.

His mother had wanted to take him, but he'd told her, "I can handle it."

The last of the snow was melting, and he had to walk through icy little streams of water. It felt very chilly that first day at the army base school. Back in Atlanta, he'd gone to a civilian school in the sunshine.

He went bravely up the steps. A man at the door told him where to find his classroom. He went directly there and laid his report card on the teacher's desk. Then he answered all of her questions. Miss Adams said, "We're glad to have you. You may choose which desk you'd like."

The classroom was small. Children rushed by him to take their seats. When all were seated, there were two empty desks.

One was by a dark-haired boy who frowned at him. The other desk was by a red-haired girl who smiled. Jonathan chose to sit by the girl. She whispered her name, Sally, and shared her books.

At recess, Miss Adams gave him his own books.

Right after recess was storytelling time. The title on the bulletin board was Native Animals and Birds. Sally told about two white rabbits her parents had given her. She had helped her father build a hutch for them.

A boy named Kent told about a trip his family had taken to a wild animal shelter. He had seen a fox and lots of other wild animals, and had bought cheese on the way home.

Two more children told about going to the same shelter. They'd also bought cheese on the way home.

Jonathan thought they were pretty nice kids. Good talkers. Maybe he was going to like this school a lot.

Miss Adams said, "Jonathan, would you like to introduce yourself to the class? Tell us who you are and where you're from."

Jonathan nodded. He'd been trying to think up some story to tell. He liked story telling. Well, actually, he loved story telling. What he had to say would fit in with the subject of native birds really well.

"I'm Jonathan and I was brought by the storks," he said proudly. "I was born right near here. But I've lived in Atlanta all my life. Storks are native to . . ."

The boy who had frowned stood up. "Storks don't bring babies! Everyone knows babies are formed inside mothers."

Jonathan's face grew hot. "I know about babies. My father's a doctor," he said. He wasn't used to having anyone stop his stories. He thought he'd better sit down.

But Miss Adams was at his side, holding him back.

"Robert! Wait your turn," she said. Then she patted Jonathan's shoulder and said, "Go on. Yours is a very interesting story."

It wasn't so easy starting up a story the second time. Of course, Jonathan knew where babies came from, but he liked the stork myth. It seemed real in its own way.

His mother had told him often of his birth. She always started with the same words: "We wanted a baby so very much. Remember that, Jonathan. You were a most wanted child."

Jonathan told the class, "I was a most wanted child."

The kids laughed. That boy, Robert, laughed the loudest. Jonathan had felt good when Mother said those words. But maybe his was a private story. Maybe he should not tell it in front of the class.

"The storks did bring me! They did! I'll prove it when the storks come again. They're going to get me a baby brother then!" he said wildly.

He hadn't meant to say that, but he had always wanted a baby brother—more than anything in the world—when he was back in Atlanta. Babies were so cute, and funnier than anything. He'd wanted to have a brother or sister to play with, like lots of his friends had. Once or twice he'd seen how Mother smiled when she handed him a friend's baby to hold. He had wanted a baby for her to love, too.

Now he wanted a brother just to have someone to like him. Little babies had always liked him. A little brother would listen to Jonathan's stories and not laugh—unless they were funny, of course.

That laughing boy, Robert, said, "Miss Adams, what he says is impossible!" Then he added, "But if a stork does bring him a brother, I'd like to be there to see it. Then I'll believe it."

The kids laughed louder. Jonathan sat down and put his head on his desk.

There, he'd done it. He'd messed up the magic of his wonderful story and made all the kids laugh at him. He hated this school! He wished he was back in Atlanta. He didn't even want to be here when the storks came. But the storks had brought him. He had to trust the storks to bring him a brother and prove him right! He'd made a promise that they would, and now he had to make it happen.

CHAPTER TWO

Jonathan tried to act calm when he got home. He even forced a smile for Mother's sake. He wouldn't tell her what had happened in school.

"How did it go at school? Did you give the teacher your report card?" Mother asked.

Jonathan nodded. He felt too awful to say a word.

"The very first day at a school is always hard," Mother said, and pulled him in close. "Say, let's have a snack. I've got a new kind of cheese. And you'll love these crackers with seeds on them."

He nodded again. Then he ate, but not much.

"Don't you want to tell me about your day, Jonathan? You're always full of stories. Come on, where's my happy Jonathan?"

"You tell me the story of when I was born," Jonathan finally said. He always felt so good when she told it. It might help.

She pulled him down on the couch next to her. "We wanted a baby so very much. Remember that, Jonathan. You were a most wanted child."

She began as she always did, and Jonathan felt better at once.

"Your father and I had been married ten years. We still had no baby. Then Dad was stationed in Germany. At this very base. But we lived in a little house outside the base."

Jonathan said, "And it had a red-tiled roof that sloped almost to the ground. We'd be in it now, but it's not for rent. It was a little different from the rest of the houses. There was a stork's nest on the roof-top! It was for the storks that brought me."

"Who's telling this story, me or you?" Mother said with a chuckle.

Jonathan always said something at this point in the story. He wanted a pause before she told the bad part. The part where his blood parents were killed in a landslide.

He listened while Mother told it and was sad again. Then he cheered up at the part where Dad was the doctor who came to the rescue.

"Dad helped you be born. Then he brought you home to me. I was to watch over you until your family was found." Mother's hands began to cup.

Jonathan finished for her. "I was a premature baby . . . very tiny. I fit in Dad's cupped hands."

"Oh, yes. You were very tiny. I was almost expecting you. The storks had just claimed our rooftop nest that day. I watched all day as they made nest repairs. They sailed through the air with bits of paper and white cloth to line the nest."

"And you thought of the old myth of how storks brought babies, and wished for one," Jonathan said.

"I did," said Mother. "I dreamed and watched until almost dark. I'd just gone inside when your father came home with you. A tiny baby wrapped in a small white square of cloth no larger than the pieces of cloth the storks carried in their bills. My dream had become real."

"And then you found my old great-uncle." Jonathan felt close to that old man who was his blood relative.

"Yes, your great-uncle lived in northern Germany. But he was too old to care for a tiny baby. He said it was best for a premature baby to live in the home of a doctor. Later Dad and the old man agreed on a private adoption."

"But it was all because the storks brought me. They did bring me?"

"Yes, indeed. And I have a surprise that proves it. Wait." She went to the shelf and took down a large white book. It was his baby book.

Mother opened it. Between the front pages

were old newspaper clippings. As always, the clippings proved her story. The papers had said he was the boy the storks brought. But that was not her surprise.

She showed him a copy of a new clipping. "Look what I found in the local library today. This was in a big city newspaper when you were born. I hadn't seen it at the time."

There was a drawn picture of a stork. A real picture of Jonathan was in the cloth the stork held.

"May I have this to take to school?" Jonathan asked. This would show the class, and that Robert! They'd see that a stork did bring him.

"Of course, if you'd like to take it," Mother said.

CHAPTER THREE

Jonathan and Mother looked at all the old news-paper clippings and the snapshots Dad had taken. Some were of the storks and their own baby.

Mother said, "You were so tiny I fed you with an eyedropper until we could get you to a hospital with an incubator and proper feeding tools. And each day I weighed you. You grew almost as fast as the stork's chick."

"The female stork laid only one egg, that's why only one chick was hatched." Jonathan put in an important detail.

"But her chick was born healthy, as healthy as you. It looked almost as bald as you, too. The stork parents cared for it. Your daddy and I cared for you. And we wrote your old uncle and sent him pictures."

Mother pointed to the picture of his great-uncle. "He wrote back saying he'd done right by you. We visited him once and he kept saying, *'Glücklich!*

Glücklich!' That meant he was very happy. We were all successful parents that summer."

Jonathan looked at a small snapshot of his blood parents that the old uncle had given him. Sometimes he wondered about them, too. But not very much. He didn't wait for the part in the story where the old uncle finally died. He put away the photos and news clippings. He folded and put the new material in his pocket. He thanked Mother by giving her a hug.

Mother sure did love babies. So Jonathan knew she was bound to love the little brother he was going to have the storks bring the family. Of course, storks couldn't really bring babies, but they could bring good luck to help you get one. He was living proof.

It could happen again. Dad would probably deliver lots of babies. And if just one turned out to be unwanted, Jonathan was sure his parents would take it home. After all, they'd done it before. And hadn't people kept saying to Mother and Dad, "You don't want Jonathan to grow up all alone. When are you going to get him a brother?"

Mother had always answered, "We're happy just to have Jonathan."

Jonathan had been happy with things as they were, too, and had never felt lonely. Of course, he'd wished for a brother. But he had lots of friends to play with back in Atlanta. Here in Germany, he had no friend. And he never was going to find a friend among those kids who had laughed at him. Every boy in the world should have at least one friend. Or a brother.

He let Mother hug him close. Let her think it was a hug for the stork story.

"I've another surprise for you today," Mother said. "Dad's taking us to see the house where we lived when you were a baby. Get ready. He'll be here soon."

Jonathan got ready and waited outside. He chucked a few hunks of old wet snow against the house. He just wanted to get a baby brother, or get on back to Atlanta. It never snowed in Atlanta.

He took the clipping out of his pocket and looked at it again. The kids would probably laugh at this silly picture. He didn't know what he could do about it. Well, at least he'd prove his story was true. They'd see.

When Mother came out, Jonathan asked, "Do storks always bring luck for a new baby?"

"In my case, it sure worked," Mother said. "It was the happiest day of my life. Luck can happen anywhere, I guess. But . . . Oh, Jonathan, Dad's here. It's time to see our old home."

Some wet snow hit Jonathan's leg. Dad came teasing for a fight. Jonathan tossed snow back.

Then Mother pushed them toward the car, all smiles. She said, "All set to see our good-luck house?"

They got into the car and drove toward his first home. Jonathan hoped a stork would arrive at the nest the very moment they got there. Then he'd know there would be a brother for him to adopt.

As they drove along, Dad kept saying how much the village had grown.

Mother kept asking where all the storks' nests had gone. "I don't see a one. Not a single one. What's happened to them?"

"We'll ask a local person, soon as we stop," Dad promised.

Mother called out, "This is it! There's the house where you lived as a tiny baby, Jonathan! Look, dear, look!"

The house looked just like the pictures, except it had a TV antenna. But before Jonathan could get a really good look, Mother screamed.

"The nest is gone! Oh, my gosh, our storks' nest is gone."

Tears came to Jonathan's eyes. "This house was supposed to be good luck. It's been hit by bad luck!" he said.

Dad said, "It's been years, Jonathan, since we were here. All things change as you grow older. Let me go ask about the nest." He got out of the car and went to the house and knocked. Dad and Mother could speak some German. Jonathan couldn't speak one word of it.

Mother patted Jonathan. "It doesn't matter, dear. This house is still your first home. I'm sorry if I sounded alarmed. It's just that storks have come to Europe every spring for millions of years. They use the same nests again and again. I hadn't expected this one to be gone. Some of the nests get huge from being added to each year."

She got out of the car and walked around to the side of the house, checking. Jonathan followed. Maybe the nest was moved to the other side.

"It's been torn down. Not even the wagon wheel is left. Oh, Jonathan, it used to be right up there on the ridgepole. Storks always pick the highest places. See the little piece of metal where the wheel was anchored?"

Jonathan couldn't see. He stretched and still could not see. He took a few steps backward and could not see. He took a few more steps backward and WHUMP! He'd crashed into someone.

Jonathan looked down into the frowning face of Robert. He had knocked down that boy from school. Talk about bad luck!

CHAPTER FOUR

"Army brat," Robert said as he got up.

Jonathan hated that name. A couple of kids in Atlanta had called him that once. They were mad and mean, and not army. But this Robert went to the school on base. "You're an army brat yourself!" Jonathan shouted back.

"Am not!"

"You are, too!"

Soon people were all around. People from the house that was Jonathan's spoke German. People from the house next door spoke English. Everyone wanted them to stop yelling.

It was Robert's mother and two little sisters who spoke English. His mother pulled Robert back inside. Jonathan was glad they hadn't moved into their old house.

The neighbors told Dad and Mother about Robert's family. His mother was an American doctor who was divorced from an army man who had returned to the United States. She'd stayed on to deliver babies for the army wives. But she was not in the army herself. She was a single parent, and that's how she made a living. Robert was the only kid in school whose parent was a civilian.

Well, there went Dad's chance of helping at births. It was not like years ago, when Dad helped with deliveries. Now Robert's mother would get any unwanted baby. That's probably how she got Robert and those two little girls. Some people had all the luck, if you could call Robert luck.

The neighbors invited Jonathan in to see his old room. Dad and Mother nodded. They all had a big slice of apple coffee cake, and Dad and Mother talked. Jonathan listened and waited for his parents to translate.

He learned why the nest had been torn down: The storks had stopped coming. There were too many telephone wires and TV antennas about. The town had grown and the stork population had decreased. Storks don't like heavy traffic. The people feared the storks were becoming an endangered species.

When they'd said good-bye and returned to the car, Jonathan said, "Too much bad luck here. Looks like we'd better go back to Atlanta right away."

"The army might frown on such fast changes,"

Dad said. "We have little choice in the matter, anyway. Hey, buddy, you'll see some storks before we leave. I'm sure of it."

Mother said, "The storks are nesting somewhere. They haven't stopped migrating."

That cheered Jonathan. "They've migrated to Europe for millions of years," he said to impress Dad.

Dad was impressed. "Yep, you've got to see the spring migration, Jonathan. That's really a fine sight."

"Oh, yes. But Jonathan must also see them nesting. Even if it's in trees," Mother said and looked at Dad. "Maybe we can visit some of the smaller villages nearby. Maybe some house will have no TV antennas."

Jonathan couldn't settle for that. "They've got to be our storks. Maybe they'll nest in trees close to our house. It'd still be our good luck. I'll get them to nest in our trees!"

Mother smiled at that. She reached across the seat to pat his shoulder, as she did sometimes when he made big claims. "What good luck are you wishing for, son?"

He'd done it. Just now he'd promised to get the storks to nest near his family, which was impossible. He didn't know how to do that. It was as impossible as what he'd told the school kids, that the storks would bring him a baby brother. Yet he wanted to believe both promises.

If only he could find how to make storks come where he wanted them, luck would follow. Stork-luck made impossible things possible. Well, he must do it.

CHAPTER FIVE

They stopped at the library to make another copy of the news clipping for Jonathan to leave at school. He looked at a book on storks. It told him nothing, at least nothing about how to make a stork nest in nearby trees, let alone on his housetop. A book called *All About Storks* was listed, but it had been checked out by someone else. Jonathan's book did tell all about how storks fly. He had to admit that was real interesting stuff. And, since storks were a native bird in Germany, he would give a report on them in class and show Robert that he knew lots of neat facts, at least.

He took the book and the news clipping to school on Monday.

The bulletin board title said Transportation: Trains, Planes, Ships. Nothing about native birds. Miss Adams changed the titles every other Monday, Sally told him. Sally was trying to be friendly, but Robert walked by without speaking. He was probably still mad at Jonathan for knocking him down. Well, Jonathan didn't care. And he didn't care about not having the chance to report lots of interesting facts on storks to show up Robert, who was so sure of his facts. Storks were nothing but bad luck, anyway.

When it was his turn to share, he said, "I pass."

He looked back at Robert, who was making a paper airplane. Robert noticed and quickly hid the plane in a book. Why, that was the same book on storks that Jonathan had! Well, if Robert hoped to prove Jonathan wrong about storks bringing him, he'd not be able to do it, either. The topic was changed and Jonathan was glad.

When Robert's turn came, he walked up front carrying the stork book. "My talk is about trains, planes, ships and storks," Robert said.

Jonathan wanted to die. Why hadn't he thought to say it like that? Now he had to listen to Robert tell all the neat things he'd wanted to tell.

"Storks don't mind living near people. Train noises or loud church bells don't bother them. That's enough about trains. Now about airplanes."

Robert opened the book and brought out the paper airplane.

"The airflow over a stork's wings is mainly from the direction it's moving. You know how you feel when you hold your hand out of a car window and angle it different ways? Well, a stork gets just the right angle between the pitch of the wing and the direction of the airstream."

Jonathan wasn't clear just what that meant, and hadn't been even when he'd read it. But Robert used the plane to show the angle he was talking about.

Jonathan wished he was not interested, but he was. In fact, he and his best friend back in Atlanta loved to explore and find out how things worked. Two boys can learn lots of things, together.

"First it's set at a very large angle like this. The stork holds his wings close in. It looks like he's coming down in a parachute." Robert crooked his arms and held them close in.

"Then he gives a twist to these stiff alula feathers." Robert held up the book jacket. He pointed to some little wing feathers. "The airstream flows around the surface of the stork's wings. The alula feathers serve as brakes like this airplane's lower flaps."

Robert had even made little flaps on the paper airplane. Jonathan groaned. He would have to check out that book *All About Storks* as soon as it was returned.

Well, at least Robert wasn't trying to prove that boys weren't brought by storks. Or that storks couldn't possibly bring Jonathan a baby brother, since no one could make storks land in a certain spot. It appeared Robert was just trying to out-story-tell him.

Well, he'd read that book, too, and was a very good storyteller himself. He waved his hand and said, "I'll take my turn after all."

Robert said, "I'm not finished. I haven't gotten to the ship part."

Miss Adams thanked him, anyway, and asked him to give others a turn. Jonathan walked up front.

"My talk is about gliders. That's a type of plane. And about ships and storks, too."

"Well," said Miss Adams, and smiled.

"You know how the sun can make sand get really hot? Or dirt even? Well, the air above the ground gets warm, too. Hot air rises. Back in Atlanta, my best friend and I did an experiment on that. I used these two balloons . . ."

"Jonathan, better not go into that now," said Miss Adams.

Jonathan felt just a little hurt at being stopped. But then she'd stopped Robert so he could have a turn. He guessed she was fair.

"Well, hot air does rise and it's called a thermal. Storks let the air carry them up. They ride

thermals! They soar around and around like this."
He stretched out his arms and soared while Robert
watched.

"They can go for miles and miles without flapping their wings. They're like gliders and hang
gliders. Storks aren't all that good at wing flapping,
but they love to soar. Now, here's the part about
ships."

"Jonathan, quickly now," Miss Adams said.

"They sometimes go over water where there are
no thermals. At first they glide, but after a while
they have to wing flap. To save energy, they swoop
down above a big ship whose deck is hot and ride
on that hot air. They're smart. That's all."

The kids liked it. They really clapped loud.
Jonathan felt wonderful. He might be able to stay
here for the entire time the army said. He pulled
the news clipping from his pocket and started to
talk more.

Miss Adams was there at once, asking him to sit
down. She saw the clipping and stopped. "Is this
you, Jonathan?"

"Yes," Jonathan said.

The class got very quiet. Miss Adams was read-
ing the print under the picture. "Well, I guess you
are the boy the storks brought," she said.

Then she went to the bulletin board. She tacked

the clipping up in a high spot, right above a ship.

"There," she said, "storks do belong on this bulletin board. You two boys have proved that. You two are a lot alike. I'll bet you'll become the best of friends."

"No!" Robert shouted.

That made Jonathan feel just awful, and right when he was feeling so good.

The recess bell rang. The kids dashed to see the news clipping. Miss Adams took Jonathan by the arm. They went to Robert's desk.

She said softly, "Robert, you'd like a good friend. I know you would. Jonathan is new and likes to tell stories like you. It seems he'd be just perfect."

"No! Every time I get a good friend, he leaves. Army brat!" Robert hissed as he laid his head on his arms.

He was crying. Jonathan could tell, even when there was no sign. He had to do something. He just had to do something.

CHAPTER SIX

Jonathan said, "Robert, you can help me get a stork to nest on my house."

Robert didn't raise his head. "No," he mumbled. He was still crying.

Jonathan didn't know anything else to say. He'd just offered his best idea. It really would be nice to have a friend to plan with, a friend who really liked storks, who knew all about storks.

"I'll listen to your stories," he offered.

"Miss Adams listens." That was all Robert said.

Jonathan waited a minute longer, but Robert never looked up. Jonathan guessed Robert really must hate him if he didn't even want to tell stories or share or anything.

Jonathan went home, sat on his back steps, and made plans alone. More than ever he wanted that baby brother now. There had to be some place where there were no antennas.

Everybody in the neighborhood had a television,

including them. No stork would nest near that many antennas. He'd never get a stork to come to their house, or even close. He was sad and even his mother looked sad.

He asked her, "Does a stork have to be on your very own house or at least in your very own neighborhood to bring luck?"

"Jonathan, honey," she said, and reached out to touch him. "Why all this need for luck?"

"I just need the storks to come, that's all. Well, do they have to actually land on your roof to bring luck?"

Mother thought for a moment. "I think they must be your storks, ones that you name. Oh, Jonathan, I'd love it if the storks came, but we have to face facts. They don't come to this town anymore. We could count it luck if the storks just touched down to feed. I hear last year they stopped at the meadow pond to feed. Where are you going, Jonathan?"

"Outside. I'm going for a walk."

Mother had gone for a walk with him several times the first week. She didn't object, but she did say, "Don't be gone long. Remember your homework. Be back before Dad gets home. Button your jacket."

The meadow belonged to the army. It was not a park. It was land the army didn't need right now but might need later. It was just sitting there past the base, a natural place for birds and small animals to be — or for a boy to mess around in. There wasn't an antenna anywhere near it.

Once a highway had gone through the meadow. Now it was all broken from lack of use and upkeep. Grass grew in the cracks. Some old telephone poles still stood, but had no wires. One brick wall of a house stood all alone. Part of it was crumbled. It had been bombed in World War II.

But the best part about that old brick wall was that it was high. Storks nest in the highest places around. Mother said so. That wall was the highest. Even the trees weren't much higher than the bushes near the pond.

There had been some big trees there once. Maybe the army or some lumberjack cut them down. Some of the stumps still stood, rotting. They made nice places for bugs and mice to hide in. Storks could find plenty of food here.

If the flock did stop to feed, and saw a nest, a pair might stay. Jonathan decided something right then. He would build a nest on top of that high brick wall.

Wow, that was the best idea in all the world. He felt so happy, he hugged an old tree stump. His arms barely went halfway around.

A rustling noise near the pond startled him. He

sat down behind the stump and waited quietly. No more sounds. His heart slowed. Native wildlife, he guessed. He got up to gather twigs.

Storks made their nest of sticks and twigs and scraps of paper and stuff like that. He'd better get some of those things carried to the top of that old brick wall.

The wall was broken in a way that made it pretty much like stairs. One place was almost a three-foot step. He had to lay his twigs on top and then get a toehold and climb up. The rest wasn't all that difficult.

He worked hard for an hour. Once he had the feeling someone was watching him. He looked all around. Nothing. He threw sticks into the tall, dry meadow grasses. Nothing came out. Native wildlife, he guessed.

Then, just as he was leaving to go home, he got that feeling again. It came really strong this time. He was sure he saw bushes by the pond move. He didn't go look, though. He just ran for home, real fast.

CHAPTER SEVEN

Jonathan worked on his nest a little each day. It took lots of work building a nest a few twigs a trip. He didn't stay late, for he kept having the feeling he was being watched.

On Monday, the title at the top of the bulletin board said Homes. Under that it said Caves, Houses, Igloos, and Tents.

Jonathan looked up "caves" in the encyclopedia. It was interesting, but his mind wasn't on bears or cave dwellers. It was on storks. It was also on the baby brother he would soon have—a brother to play with and take care of, to listen to his stories and think him terrific.

He went to the library to see if the book *All About Storks* was in.

The librarian said, "I'm sorry. The book did come in, but it was checked out right away. We really should order another copy, I guess. I'll bet we can find something in an old *National Geographic*."

It was a pretty good article in the *National Geographic*. But it didn't tell as much as a book. There was hardly anything at all about storks' nests.

Jonathan felt sad. Rather than go home with nothing, he checked out another book. It was all about snakes. He read it the rest of the day. He didn't feel like going back to work on his stork's nest.

At the next sharing time at school, Jonathan got up first. He loved to talk and he had something to say. That *National Geographic* article wasn't all that bad.

"I'd like to tell you about caves, houses, igloos, tents, and storks' nests. Millions of years ago, storks maybe lived in caves. High ones, up in the cliffs."

Already Robert was waving his hand for a turn.

"And later they nested in high trees," Jonathan said. He wished Robert would stop that waving. Robert just wanted to show him up, and he knew it. It was probably Robert who'd checked out that book. He'd make sure he covered *all* the topics before he sat down. That would show Robert!

"Then people came on the earth. The storks liked people a lot. People liked them a lot, too.

Storks kept neighborhoods free of mice and snakes. Now they nest on housetops. I really wanted some storks to come to our housetop, like when I was born."

"Impossible!" Robert shouted.

Miss Adams shushed him. Jonathan continued, "I guess storks never lived in igloos. Storks like warm weather. That's why they migrate. They come to Europe when it's warm. Then go back to Africa when it's warm down there."

He paused. What could he say about tents? Oh, let Robert hit tents. He sat down. Robert ran up front. He was carrying a book. It was *All About Storks*!

"The storks' homes are their nests. I'll tell you about some great ones. I read all about them in this book," Robert began.

He told about one old nest that had been added to year after year. It weighed over one hundred pounds. It was more than six feet across. And it was several feet high. It was so heavy the rooftop almost caved in, so the people had to tear part of it away. Robert's talk was so interesting, Jonathan's heart began to thump real loud. He wished he didn't dislike Robert so much. But Robert hated him, so Jonathan had to dislike him.

Next Robert listed the different bases people made for the storks' nests. Wagon wheels. The bottoms and stays of old barrels. Special little platforms.

Jonathan's heart really thumped after that statement. He hadn't made a base to hold the nest he'd started. Robert knew too much. It wasn't fair.

"Build a real good base for a nest, and the storks will use it year after year," Robert was saying.

Miss Adams let Robert talk too long. Maybe he was her pet. It wasn't fair. Even if the kids all begged him to tell more, it still wasn't fair.

Jonathan ran all the way home from school. He stuck his head inside and called to Mom, "I'm going for a walk!"

"Jonathan, you just got home. Oh, all right. It is getting warmer out. I guess it's time the outdoors claims you for the summer."

Away he ran again, heading straight for the meadow. He'd have to look things over real good. And plan how to make a platform for the stork's nest.

Once he got near the brick wall, he stopped short. There was a base under his stork's nest already! It was the bottom of an old barrel. The stays were sort of spread out. But they stuck up just enough so the sticks held nicely in place. It was a really good base, and Jonathan knew the guy who had done it! Robert, who hated him! Robert showing him up again. Why couldn't Robert forget fighting and be friends?

Jonathan's lips got tight from the hurt. His heart raced, and then his feet moved. He ran to Robert's house. Robert came to the door. He held a half-eaten cookie in one hand, a glass of milk in the other.

Jonathan said, "I'm the boy the storks brought. That was my nest. Stay away from it! The storks that'll come will be my storks, not yours! And they're going to bring me a little brother, not you!" He turned away, then ran.

Still he heard Robert say, "It was impossible, the way it was built!" and heard him slam the door.

CHAPTER EIGHT

Jonathan never spoke to Robert during school. He worked on the nest every day after school, alone. Robert never came spying again. That was just fine. Jonathan needed no help from Robert. Even if he had kept the base, the nest was really all his.

Next week the bulletin board said Foods at the top. Underneath, it said Meat, Dairy, Vegetables, and Grain.

Jonathan had planned to tell how storks ate snakes, bugs, toads, fish, and mice. All that was meat. It would fit in fine.

Miss Adams let Sally show a food chart she'd made. Sally talked really long. Then her best friend, Erika, got equal time. Kent got a turn next. Jonathan was hardly listening and didn't notice when Kent stopped.

Robert didn't miss the finish. He went right up front in a hurry. He was going to give a report about infertile eggs. "It's about how infertile eggs won't hatch. Some storks' eggs never hatch because they're infertile. My mother says . . ."

"Robert, keep to the topic. Food," said Miss Adams.

"Storks need proper food to be healthy. My mother says the body has to work just right, or else eggs may not even be laid. People's bodies have to work just right or they can't have babies, either. My mother has helped lots of women so they can have babies. But some women never can."

"Robert. Medical science is interesting, but we're talking about food."

Miss Adams didn't make him sit down, though she should have.

Robert said, "Even if someone should build a good nest, it's likely the storks won't claim it. They have to be near a good food supply. This book says so." Robert waved *All About Storks*.

Then he added, "I really hope storks do come and stay. If they do, it would be so great it'd be in all the newspapers. I'd like to help make sure the storks have a good food supply." Robert looked straight at Jonathan. It was a friendly look. Jonathan was almost certain.

Jonathan had already been thinking hard about the food supply. So after school, he went to the pond. He was not surprised to see Robert there, poking around. He wanted to say hi, but Robert didn't say it first.

Without speaking, they began working together, Jonathan on one side of the pond, Robert on the other. Jonathan made some little stepping-stones go out into the pond. He didn't look up, but he said, "This is just in case the storks need to be in deeper water to catch fish."

"Their legs are plenty long. They can wade out far enough," Robert said, sort of cross, like he hated to be friendly. Then he added, "That's what the book said."

"Oh, yeah," said Jonathan. It wasn't fair that Robert knew so much—unless he was a friend. Robert began throwing sticks into a narrow outlet of water like mad.

"Just what do you think you're doing?" Jonathan asked because he didn't know. And because it could mean Robert was really mad.

"I'm building a dam so the tadpoles will stay all in one place. That way they won't get eaten and will grow. Storks like frogs."

"I know that," said Jonathan, relieved. Robert wasn't mad at all. "That's not a bad start for a dam. I can show you how to build a great dam."

He really did know how. He and his best friend had dammed up lots of little creeks when he'd lived in Atlanta.

He gathered sticks and stones. Then he got chunks of sod, some old dry grass, and mud.

"That's a pretty good dam," said Robert, and started doing the same.

"Yeah," said Jonathan. And helped Robert top off the dam with more dry grass, just for looks.

"Wanta stop over for milk and cookies?" asked Robert. "My sitter bakes great cookies."

"Sure," said Jonathan.

"It's getting pretty close to the time for the stork migration," Robert said.

"Yeah. Sure is. But we'll have things ready when they get here! Won't we?" said Jonathan, and stopped short. Supposing the storks did come, would it make any difference if Robert had helped bring them? Would the storks know it was Jonathan who wanted a baby brother and not Robert?

But surely having a friend who really loved storks and wanted them back couldn't possibly spoil Jonathan's luck. The baby would be his, for he'd started this project. And when he got that new baby brother, he and Robert could still be friends and play together. They could take the kid along.

CHAPTER NINE

Springtime came suddenly. One morning the meadow and trees had a tint of green. The sun shone bright. The sky got blue with low white cloud puffs.

There in the meadow, just past the army base, the boy the storks brought stood. He waited. His friend Robert stood beside him. They were near the old and broken brick wall. Hiding.

A great flock of storks soared high above the clouds.

Like shadows in the sky, they flew in very slow movement. Long, graceful necks were extended. A great clattering noise moved along with them.

"The sounds come from the storks clapping their bills," Robert whispered.

"I know that," said Jonathan. "You think they're going to come down?"

"The noise is getting louder."

"They are coming! They are coming right here!"

Jonathan scrunched down. He hid real low in the tall grass at the end of the wall. Robert did the same. They did not talk. Just watched.

There were hundreds and hundreds of storks! Jonathan had never seen so many birds in one place. Their feathers glowed white in the sun. Their red bills and legs were like a bright crayon touch, finishing off a pretty picture.

Jet-black-tipped wings spread wide, and feet reached out. They landed!

The boys held tight to the grass, so as not to be noticed. They didn't want to think it was all a dream.

For the longest time, they said not a word.

The storks ate crickets and grasshoppers. Their landing had stirred up plenty. Some even caught toads, mice, and small snakes. Some waded out into the pond. Then widespread wings threw shadows over the water as the storks caught minnows and tadpoles. Then they stopped for a sunbath.

"They're resting," Jonathan whispered.

"Yeah, they're tired. They've come thousands of miles. Look, they're fixing their flight feathers. They're cleaning away all the dirt and stuff," Robert said.

Robert wasn't being a show-off. He was just telling Jonathan things Jonathan wanted to know.

The storks had begun to nibble at their feathers. They drew them between their beaks. That made them nice and straight once more. Then they stroked them back into place. At last, a little shake and a few wing beats settled everything properly.

Their rest and feeding stop was over. They became noisy again.

Suddenly, long legs bent and bodies jerked up sharply. A few strong wing flaps and they were in the air. They rose from the ground as neatly as a helicopter. Again the sky was filled with soaring storks.

Jonathan let out a little cry, for the beauty of it, for the fact that they were leaving.

Robert pulled up the tuft of grass he'd been gripping. "They're off to Denmark, I guess," he said, and threw away the grass.

Jonathan stood up. There was no use hiding anymore. All the storks were gone. He said, "You'd think at least two could have stayed. They never even came near my . . . the nest."

But he couldn't stop watching them. Nor could Robert. They were so graceful. Soaring around and around on a high thermal, up, up they went. Out of sight. With them went Jonathan's hope for a baby brother. He groaned.

"I wanted it to work. But I didn't ever think it was

going to work," Robert said. "Storks like people, but people can't make them do anything."

Jonathan heard a sound. He grabbed Robert and turned him around. He pointed at a small movement of grass.

It was by the water's edge, near the dam, right where an old tree root stuck up from the water. It was where Jonathan had put the last pile of grass.

They both ran.

A stork was caught in the pile of marsh grass. Its wings beat in a lopsided way.

"Robert, look! He's got an arrow through his body!"

Robert had the most puzzled look. "How'd that happen? People can't shoot arrows at storks. It's against the law!"

"In Africa it's not. It doesn't matter. Help me get him out of that mess." Jonathan was inching closer.

"It's the arrow that's caught. He can't get untangled. Don't act scared. Don't act scared," Robert said and came close, too.

But Jonathan was scared. When he was close enough to help, the stork nipped his hand. That bill was as powerful as pliers, but he had to do something to free him. Quickly. "We'd better call the police," Jonathan said.

CHAPTER TEN

Robert had gotten close, too. He missed the nip, but now he agreed with Jonathan. "Yeah, I think we'd better call the police."

"No. No! I have a better idea. I'll run home and get Mom, and she'll call Dad. Dad will take the arrow out. It'll be our family's stork. Our luck. I found him!"

"You'll have to set him free. You can't make storks stay where they don't want to stay, but I guess he better not go free with that arrow still in him." Robert was walking in circles as he talked.

"Let's build a tent over him, so he won't go away until he's fixed up."

"That's a neat idea, Jonathan. Wait until Miss Adams hears."

It didn't take long. They placed sticks in a wigwam shape over the stork. They'd learned how to in the Homes unit at school.

Robert said, "I'm calling my mom, too. Your dad may be busy. She can do surgery if she has to." Each boy ran to his own parent to get help.

Jonathan and his mother were already at the pond by the time his dad got there. Dad arrived before Robert's mother, because he was on the base. He drove his van on the old broken-up highway. He had a strong net, like a butterfly net, only bigger.

Soon Robert came with some newspaper people. He explained, "My mom was delivering a baby and couldn't come. I thought about calling the police, but I didn't. I called the newspaper. I've always wanted my picture in the newspaper for something. This is something. This is real news. You've already had a turn, Jonathan."

It was big news. Robert's little sisters and their baby-sitter came. The baby-sitter was pregnant and couldn't run fast. The neighbors across from the meadow came. Everybody was talking at once. Cameras were pointed first at this person and then at that one and then back at the stork.

There were plenty of men to help Dad hold down the stork until he could give the stork a shot. Dad said after a close look, "I do believe it is an African's arrow. My boy was right about that."

Over and over the question was asked, "How

could it possibly fly all the way from Africa with an arrow through its body?"

"Storks are strong birds," Jonathan said, and Robert agreed. The news people from the army base paper made notes. The boys told them all they needed to know about storks.

Dad took the stork back to the van and removed the arrow. "There, a little medicine and packing, and he'll be fine."

"How does the man know the stork's a he," one of Robert's sisters asked him.

Robert answered, "The male usually comes to the nests first."

Right then another car came bouncing along the old roadway. It was Robert's mother. "You're too late," Robert called. When she came near, he told her all that had happened.

"Well, I'm not too late to get in on the excitement. Wow, what a day! I just finished delivering triplets! These fertility methods!" she said, and smiled at the grown-ups.

"That's what doctors are for, to bring life and to spare life," Dad said. Then he asked, "Aren't you the family who lives next to our old place?"

Jonathan and Robert said, "Yes." Their parents laughed.

"I think we'd better get to know each other,"

Mom said. "We could have been neighbors if the house had been for rent. Our boys seem to be the best of friends. Would you care to come back to our house to visit now?"

Robert's mom nodded. "If my girls and Janice may come, too."

"Sure," answered Jonathan. "My little brother will always go along where I go."

Jonathan's mother said, "What? What . . ."

"What are you going to do with the stork?" Robert's mother interrupted.

"Put him in the nest!" said Jonathan and Robert together.

They pointed and everyone looked at the nest they'd built.

With a little help, Dad placed the stork in the nest. He said, "When he wakes up, he might choose to stay. You boys think you can find some food for him?"

Of course they could. As soon as everyone left, they used the net to catch nine minnows. Jonathan got a wet foot. Robert got scratched by a berry vine, but that was nothing. They proudly laid the fish at the edge of the nest.

When the bird started to wake, the thanks he gave them was to nip at them. They got down in a hurry. "I thought storks liked people," Jonathan said.

"Well, maybe not when they just wake up. My mom's like that," said Robert.

"Let's hide so he won't be scared," said Jonathan.

They hid and waited.

With effort the stork stood up. Then, slowly, he tested his legs, walking around the nest. He poked at spots here and there. When he came to the fish, he ate every one of them.

A black raven flew overhead and cawed a welcome or a warning. Jonathan didn't know which.

"He'll take care of himself," Jonathan said.

"Yeah," said Robert, "storks are strong birds."

The stork stood on the edge of the nest. Then he seemed to drop off the edge and went soaring. He landed to pick up a tissue that Robert's sister had dropped. Then back to the nest he flew.

First Jonathan giggled. Then Robert. "He doesn't like the nest we built," Jonathan said.

"Yeah, he thinks he can do a better job," Robert said, and giggled again.

The newspaper gave them both credit for building a good nest and for getting a stork to stay in their town. It also said: "Males usually arrive first to claim a nest. It remains to be seen if he will attract a female. All those who believe in magic, clap your hands."

Jonathan folded up the paper and slapped his hand with it. He wanted this magic to happen so badly. He just knew Mother and Dad would be so happy to have a baby. They'd sure loved him when he was a baby. He felt luck was already a certainty. Almost.

How disappointing it would be if the female didn't come. People can't make storks do anything they don't want. Not even the male could make a female choose to be his mate. His stork could be bypassed.

Big tears started to roll down Jonathan's cheeks, but he wiped them away with his sleeve. Then he clapped his hands for magic.

CHAPTER ELEVEN

"This is my kind of day. I feel something great is going to happen," Mother said. She had said those very words the day she and Dad had taken him to see a real castle. The castle was great, but nothing compared to the storks landing and the male stork being rescued. Nothing!

"Jonathan, would you put the yellow plates out on the patio table, please? I've asked Robert's mother over for lunch." Jonathan didn't mind that, or helping, but today was Saturday. He'd planned to spend all day near his stork.

"Can I go now?" he asked once the plates were down.

"Of course not. There are glasses to put out. And punch to make. Robert and the girls are coming, too. You stay home and be a good host. I'll bake a pizza for you kids. You can eat in the kitchen or out on the grass."

The phone rang. Mother took the call. "That was

Robert's mother. The girls are begging to go to a German movie with their sitter. She has promised to translate when needed and to give them a huge tub of popcorn instead of lunch. Take the girls' and the sitter's plates from the table, dear. You and Robert get a whole pizza, I guess. Maybe he can teach you a few words of German while you eat it." She laughed.

"Okay, a little," Jonathan said about learning German. Robert usually spoke only English. Jonathan had more admiration for a sitter who favored popcorn over a regular lunch. He wished he had the nerve to refuse to come to a luncheon that he didn't want to attend. He pressed Mom for a favor of his own. "Could you bake the pizza right away? Robert and I could take it out to the meadow. Then we could eat it there for lunch."

"Cold pizza. No!"

"I love cold pizza. Robert will, too. Robert's mother is letting the girls skip being here."

"Jonathan, dear, you're too eager to be with that stork. I'm afraid you're going to be awfully hurt if your stork fails to get a mate. Just be happy that one stork is living in your nest."

"But it takes a pair of storks to bring me luck!"

"Jonathan, that's enough. You're making too big of a deal of this. You are a lucky boy already. You've two parents who love you. You've a good home. I don't know what it is you want. You can't expect to be entirely spoiled in the way Janice spoils those little girls. Oh, I forget she's only a teenager her-self. Jonathan, just help me around the house till noon. Okay?" So, to make her happy, he helped Mom get ready for her luncheon.

At noon, he and Robert burned their mouths on the hot pizza, eating too fast. Then they were off to the meadow.

The stork wasn't in or near the nest.

It was awful. The stork had left them. They should have eaten cold pizza.

"I wanted to come out earlier. I just knew some-thing bad was going to happen," Jonathan said.

"I know," said Robert. "I knew it, too. A female usually comes within a week after a male claims a nest. It's been a week and one da-a-a-y." He stopped. Their stork soared in just over their heads.

The stork didn't seem to mind that they were there. He landed on the edge of the nest. Then he stood there on one leg and looked around, but mostly he looked up.

"I hear it! I hear storks clattering!" Jonathan whispered.

"A second migratory flock!" said Robert.

The stork in the nest was making a lot of noise. He was still looking at the sky. The boys did the same. This flock was as awesome as the last. Best of all, one stork cut away from the flock.

At first it looked like just a speck. Then the speck grew bigger and bigger, coming steeply downward.

"It's a female. I know it is. Just listen to the racket our stork's making!" Jonathan said out loud. There was no need to whisper. The male stork was clattering so loud he could be heard for miles.

"Yep! He's beaming her in!" shouted Robert.

She appeared to drop from the sky. When close, the underside of her wings started the braking action. Then came a downstroke of her wings. An upstroke. The beginning of another downstroke. Her legs stretched forward and she gently landed.

"What a racket! What a greeting!" sang Jonathan.

"You see the male throw back his head? You know what that means." Robert nudged Jonathan.

Of course Jonathan had seen his stork's head go back until his crown touched his back. And heard him rattle his bill louder than ever and make another deep head bow forward and clatter still more. Of course Jonathan knew it meant he was telling the female she was welcome.

She cocked her head, bowed, did some half turns, and clattered right back. Next she spread her wings a bit in a showy way.

"I thought she was going to hug him," said Robert, and giggled.

"She's choosing him, all right! We got us a stork pair, Robert!" Jonathan was almost dancing himself.

Jonathan was so happy. If the truth were known, he hadn't just wanted these storks to get a baby brother. First, he was glad for the male stork's sake. He'd got himself a mate. Second, he was glad for himself—the boy the storks brought. The storks were here, just like on the day he was born!

He had dreamed of really seeing a pair of storks in their nest. It was the unknown things about his adoption that made Jonathan feel strange and hurt sometimes. He understood he could never see his blood parents—they'd always be just a dream. But these storks he could see. They were real. They were the good-luck makers that had got him some new, loving parents. He couldn't get enough of watching.

"Now look what they're doing!" Jonathan nudged Robert this time. The storks had soared off to the pond.

"She's hungry," Jonathan decided.

"No," said Robert. "She's getting stuff to fix up the nest some more. Well, who cares? They can build it six feet across and three feet high. I don't

mind. The nest can take it. It's got a good base."

Jonathan was still a little jealous about that base, but that was done before he and Robert were friends. "Let 'em build it a mile high if they want."

"No way! We want to be able to see into the nest. We have to see how many eggs get laid. And see how many chicks hatch," Robert said. "Oh, look, there're some people. Let's go tell them to stay back."

The people were not coming too close. They had just gathered to watch, they said. They'd heard the flock. They'd seen the female drop from the sky. No one could miss the noise. The whole town knew. The whole army base knew.

"Yep, she was pretty good," said Jonathan. "She dropped better than a parachute!"

"And she landed better than a hang glider," said Robert and added some words in German for those not from the army base.

"We've got to give the pair names," said an old woman in broken English. "Just because they took up housekeeping in the meadow doesn't mean they can't be named. We always named our storks, back when they used to come to our houses."

"They have names already. I've named the female Ann," Jonathan said quickly. He didn't want anyone else giving his stork a name. No one else could claim them.

"Oh, and who's it named for, sonny? Your mother?"

Jonathan thought fast. He didn't know why he'd said Ann. It was short and had just come out quickly. "No. My mother's name is Sandra. I had a teacher back in Atlanta named Ann." That was true, and he was pleased with that explanation. Still, he guessed he really should have named the stork for Mother.

"I really liked that teacher," he added. And that was true, too; he had.

"I named the male stork Adams," said Robert.

So Robert had caught on about the instant need for naming the storks. Jonathan knew the name was for Miss Adams. But he didn't say anything. And Robert didn't explain.

"Did you say Adam, or Adams?" a woman with a note pad asked. It was a woman from the newspaper. A policeman near the crowd's edge was asking people to leave and not disturb the stork pair.

"Adam," said Robert, and walked away. "Want to play Monopoly?" he said to Jonathan.

As they walked, Jonathan said, "I don't think Miss Adams will mind. It's okay if you named the male stork after her. I knew a girl who was named Alana after her dad. She didn't mind. What you turning red for? Miss Adams your girl friend?"

"I like her a lot," Robert croaked.

CHAPTER TWELVE

At the top of the bulletin board on Monday was one word: Storks. "If you can't fight 'em, join 'em," Miss Adams said. "You boys wanted a unit on storks—you've got it."

All the kids clapped. Jonathan and Robert clapped the loudest.

At one end of the display was a piece of white paper. This question was on it: What do you call baby storks?

Some answers had already been written. Storklets. And under that: Here, storkie. Here, storkie. And under that: Get it? And under that: Adamette.

Everyone on the base had read the English edition of the Sunday newspaper.

A picture of Ann and Adam was on the front page. The entire page was tacked to the bulletin board.

One kid asked, "You doing this unit because one stork got named for you, Miss Adams?"

Robert turned red again.

"Could be," said Miss Adams. Robert smiled.

"Together we'll keep track of their nesting and hatching," Miss Adams said. "And anyone who wants can put up pictures, real or drawn. Or written stories on storks. Whatever. Just don't change the subject. Okay?"

She looked straight at Jonathan. "If anyone wants to write out the stork myth about bringing babies . . . Well, that's okay, too."

That teacher really deserved having a stork named for her, Jonathan felt. He'd be glad to do the myth story. He'd do it in cursive even. He'd draw a picture of the female with his baby brother's picture in the bundle. But two days had gone by and there'd been no baby suddenly needing adoption. He plain didn't understand it.

He hoped no one would bring it up.

Sally did. "You said you were going to prove something to us, Jonathan. Now keep your promise, Jonathan. Take a picture of the stork bringing you a baby brother, Jonathan."

The kids laughed and laughed. Jonathan felt hot.

"I will," he told them. He didn't write the myth story, or anything.

More days passed and the storks brought no miracle baby to his family. Things were not working the way they had when he was born. He couldn't just give up believing the storks would bring luck. Hadn't it been he who had found the male? Hadn't it been his father who had removed the arrow?

Jonathan decided luck would happen when their chicks were born. That was it. That explained everything. Surely.

Robert's was the first story tacked to the bulletin board. It was about nesting.

He told how Adam and Ann had added hard sticks to their nest and even an old rusty nail. How they padded the inside of the nest with soft things. Leaves. Bits of paper. Bits of cloth.

How they'd used mud as mortar. How Adam and Ann always greeted each other noisily.

Jonathan had seen all that along with Robert. They'd climbed some old telephone poles nearby to watch. One pole was leaning against the other. It made climbing easy.

Together they'd watched the mating. Adam's and Ann's beaks were crackling like fire that day. They were doing a lot of wing spreading, head cocking, and bowing.

The mating was done quickly. She switched her tail feathers to one side and he turned his tail downward. "He's planting his sperm. The eggs Ann lays will be fertile," Robert whispered.

"Good," said Jonathan.

Robert kept on explaining things his mother had told him. Most of it Jonathan already knew, but he didn't complain. He was just happy the time had come for making baby storks.

Other birds were nesting, too, in the trees and in grasses on the ground. A jackdaw even holed in in the basement part of the storks' nest. Everything was nesting. Hornets nested under the eaves of Jonathan's house.

The crab apple tree in Jonathan's yard bloomed the day Ann laid the first egg. It was hard to get a really good look at the egg. Jonathan was high enough on the telephone pole, but Ann kept the egg close under her breast to keep it warm. When she turned it over to warm the other side, Jonathan saw it was big and white.

She stayed on the nest all day. Adam brought her food.

The next day there was another egg.

Jonathan knew storks usually lay three or four eggs. Some even lay six. Some one or two, or none. Ann laid only two eggs. She sat on the eggs and kept them warm for five weeks.

It was the longest five weeks of Jonathan's life. He tried not to worry so much about whether a chick would hatch or not, or whether some other bird might steal an egg to eat. Also, he tried not to worry about whether a baby boy would be put up for adoption.

The jackdaws, which lived in the bottom edge of the storks' nest, were stealers. They put their beaks into the big nest so much, the rusty nail dropped to the ground.

Only Jonathan saw that. He picked it up and sneaked the rusty nail into Robert's desk as a joke. Was Robert ever surprised. Jonathan told him it had got there by magic.

The next day it magically got into Jonathan's lunch box. And the next day Jonathan sneaked it into Robert's gym bag. Then Jonathan found it in his math book. So it went, helping make the five weeks go past.

Jonathan and Robert shared the book *All About Storks*. Jonathan read it twice. He could just imagine how the egg shell was getting thinner and thinner. The little chicks were using the lime to build bones. But they had better not hatch during school hours. Jonathan wanted to be there to see it all, just as he wanted to be on hand when his dad came with a new baby cupped in his hands.

CHAPTER THIRTEEN

I t was a Saturday morning. Jonathan went early, climbed the pole, and watched Adam soar. As soon as the sun heated the ground and hot air began to rise, Adam rode that air. There was nothing so beautiful as a stork soaring on a thermal of hot air.

That is, except seeing a baby chick peck its way out of a shell. Out came the little dark beak. Then the shell was forced wide open. There the chick stood on wobbly dark legs. A soft wind brought the down to a fluff.

It was a beautiful sight. Jonathan wished Robert was there to share it. Robert did not show up at all.

Jonathan sat quietly, alone, with his big news. He thought how he'd share it with Mother. He waited and watched for a long time. He'd give luck a chance to work its magic before he got home. Maybe the new baby was there already. Mother would think it was a surprise for him. Ha!

The chick was born hungry. Mother had said
Jonathan took a whole bottle the first time she fed
him when he got home from the hospital. Adam
flew back to the pond for food several times.

Two baby raccoons fought in the bushes nearby,
growling, stalking, then growling some more.
They stopped only to bare their teeth and make
their fuss-fuss sounds. Just the way Robert and
Jonathan used to fight. Then they played together.

Just where was Robert, anyway? Jonathan
couldn't wait around much longer, because
Mother would worry, new baby or no. He ran
home to ease her worry.

Mother wasn't even home. She'd left a note saying she was at the hospital. That was not an unusual
note. She went there sometimes to see Dad. Today
might mean a new baby was orphaned, and Mom
had to go get it.

Jonathan sat and waited some more. He waited
for the phone call saying he had a new baby
brother.

The phone rang. It was Robert saying he was
stuck with baby-sitting. The sitter had gone to the
hospital with his mom.

Jonathan told him about the egg. And about the
raccoons. "You don't think they would steal the
chick, do you, Robert?"

"Ann wouldn't let any animal or anything do

that. I just know she wouldn't," Robert said.

"Yeah, storks are strong," Jonathan said.

The phone rang again. It was Mother saying, "I'll be a little late. And, Jonathan, we've a little surprise for you. Oh, and start supper, would you, son?"

"Sure. Sure," said Jonathan. He almost died right then and there. Gee, it must have been a surprise for Mother, too. Good gosh, they didn't even have anything ready for the baby.

Jonathan put a comforter on the floor and folded some sheets on top of it. That would have to do for a baby bed until they had time to buy a crib. Wait until he told the kids at school!

Jonathan was so excited, he totally forgot to boil some pasta. That's what he always made, macaroni and cheese. He didn't think of it until Mother walked in through the door.

It was not a baby in her arms but a big round of cheese.

"Your father got a call to go to the next town and I went along. We stopped at this great cheese factory on the way home. What's the comforter doing on the floor, Jonathan?"

Jonathan thought he would hate cheese for the rest of his life. He wouldn't even eat macaroni and cheese. He didn't love it anymore. He put the comforter on his bed and slept on it himself.

He worried all night that the first chick might get

killed. He worried that the second egg might not hatch. Things like that happened. He wished he'd never read *All About Storks*.

Then a good thought floated in that let him fall asleep with a smile. The other egg might hatch just fine. Maybe the magic would take place when it did. Maybe tomorrow would be the day a baby brother came to them.

CHAPTER FOURTEEN

The next day was Sunday. Mother and Dad said Jonathan could go watch the second chick be born. Stay all day if need be. He called Robert and he was free to go, too. They packed their lunch— no cheese—and left.

They climbed up the telephone poles, but they'd arrived there too late for the show. Two chicks were in the nest, mouths open. Both were alive and healthy! The first one seemed much taller than the new one.

Adam was standing guard at the edge of the nest. It took a while for Jonathan to spot Ann in the marsh nearby.

Her long neck, like a periscope, stuck above the marsh grass. She speared a small snake and ate it. Then she got two frogs and another little snake.

Then her knees bent and she rushed into the air and was off toward an open field. The ground had warmed enough so she could soar. She caught and ate four mice.

Back to the nest she came. The babies grew silent. They sat with beaks pointed toward the center of the big nest. Adam and Ann got noisy, clattering bills in greeting. With head cocking and bowing, they changed guards. Then Adam flew off for his turn to gather food.

The babies started pecking at their mother's bill.

She stood directly above them. Her neck stretched and stiffened. She threw up the food she'd eaten. The chicks pecked, pulled, and fought over the pieces.

It was something to see. Jonathan decided he loved all nature.

The sun was up higher, the thermals nice. Adam rode one thermal, then soared to the next. Around and above the rocks he soared, landing only to eat lizards and toads until his craw grew heavy and fat.

Ann guarded her nest and preened her feathers with her bill. To clean her neck and head, she used her foot.

Adam caught eleven spring frogs. Robert counted. "Protein builds muscles," he said. "Hey, I'm getting hungry."

As the boys ate their sandwiches, they talked about names.

"We can't name them now. We don't know if they are male or female," said Robert.

"We could change the names later," Jonathan said. "Mother said she had a girl's name picked, just in case I was a girl."

"I thought you were adopted. How could she have a name picked?" asked Robert.

"Well, she did. She had picked out two names in case she had the chance to adopt a baby."

"How does it feel to be adopted, Jonathan?"

"I don't really think about it much."

"Don't you wish you knew your real parents?" Robert asked.

Jonathan took the question seriously and answered, "I think it'd make me feel too sad. I look at their picture sometimes."

"Sometimes I wish I could see my father," Robert said. "I don't hardly remember what he looks like. He lives back in the States now." Robert sat there looking sad.

"I guess adoption feels something like that. You got a picture of your dad?"

"Yeah, and I got my mother here in person. And my sisters."

"Yeah, it's like that. I'm glad my Mother and Dad are here to love me, too. And feed me." He motioned toward the baby storks being fed again.

"You eat lizards?" Robert said, and gagged in a silly way.

"I've got a picture of my blood parents, and of my old great-uncle. He was neat. Know what his name was? Friedrich. Want to name one of the stork babies Friedrich?" Jonathan asked, and then he got a better idea. "We could run a name-the-storks contest at school."

He felt he was being a really good sport, giving his school friends a chance to name the storks. He already had a name picked for his baby brother and it wasn't Friedrich.

Robert liked the name-contest idea. They talked on and on about it, until it got to be late afternoon, then Robert said, "We'd better stop talking and get home."

"Not yet," said Jonathan. "I'm waiting . . ." He wanted to tell Robert he was giving stork-luck time to work again. Well, Robert was his best friend ever, and they'd just shared some private things. So he told him all.

This time Robert didn't say Jonathan's dream was impossible. He just waited with Jonathan until almost dark. Then they ran like mad to Jonathan's house to see the new baby.

CHAPTER FIFTEEN

Next day, two hundred and fifty names were put on the name-the-chick list at school. Jonathan could have vetoed the name he'd saved for his brother. It didn't matter. No baby was up for adoption, anyway.

Everyone wrote the names of his or her sisters and brothers, mothers and fathers, aunts and uncles. Jonathan did what he could. He added Friedrich. Then Sally cheated and brought a name list. She stood by the bulletin board for an hour, adding names.

A man had come to band the chicks, so they'd know if they returned the next year. He said the larger chick was male, the other female. So now names could be given.

Miss Adams insisted on a secret vote. The names Violet and Victor won. Sally had been telling everyone to vote that way. Jonathan had hoped for

Robert or Sandra or Friedrich, but fair was fair. He called them Violet and Victor.

That got into the newspaper, too. Robert and Miss Adams saw to it.

The chicks grew rapidly each day.

The chicks got feathers. They flapped wings to build muscles. They practiced short flights inside the nest. As summer came and went, they soloed and turned into young adults. The air got cooler in late August. Then one day it was time for them to join the flock headed for Africa.

Jonathan and Robert watched as the twin storks and their parents rode some high thermal around and around, up and up. Finally, they were with the flock, lost from sight.

"They'll come back next year. Lots of storks claim their old nests. Maybe Ann and Adam will," said Robert.

Jonathan said, "And maybe if we start another nest . . . I'll make a really good base for it. Maybe Violet and Victor will come back and get mates. Then we'll have six storks. Maybe with that many, luck will really happen."

School started again in September. The kids forgot that Jonathan had made a promise he never kept. Miss Adams kept changing the titles on the bulletin board. There was a new subject every other week. Jonathan and Robert had to read lots of books, maybe a hundred, about lots of things. Some facts, some myths.

They read them together when Robert slept over. Jonathan's parents weren't ready yet to let him stay at Robert's house. He knew they thought he was too young. Robert's mother considered Robert older because he was older than his sisters. Some kids had all the luck.

Robert quoted some new facts he'd read. Jonathan told about myths he liked best. Jonathan guessed he'd always sort of believe in luck and the magic of things. Maybe when the storks came back . . . But no. By next spring Mother would have her fortieth birthday. She'd be too old to adopt a baby. He tried to forget about having a brother and just be happy that Robert was sleeping over.

CHAPTER SIXTEEN

Jonathan and Robert were awakened just before daybreak. Robert's mother dashed in with the two little girls still in their nightgowns. She said to Jonathan's mother, "It's one thing to deliver babies for others. But when it's the sitter, where do I leave my children?"

Mother and Dad helped situate the sleepy girls on the couch, foot to foot. "There," said Mother, "they can finish the night here just fine. You don't need to worry about a thing."

Robert's mom said, "I'm afraid I do. I just found out the dear girl has not called her aunt, who is to adopt. Not for six months!"

Robert shouted. "Janice is having her baby tonight? Why didn't anyone tell me?"

Jonathan had his own demand to make. "Why didn't you tell me you had a baby at your house to be adopted? Robert, I told you I wanted a brother! You knew!"

The grown-ups drew in their breaths and let it out in What? What? sounds.

Dad pulled the boys from each other. "Sh-h-h. Back to bed, you two, and finish out your night, as well." Jonathan heard no more, not even the slam of the door. He was too furious to listen to anything, not even to Robert's worried talk.

"I don't know who will be our sitter now. Friends leave. Everybody leaves around here. Janice was good. She kept the girls out of my things. She and Mom made a trade: a place to stay and medical care in return for her tending my sisters. She's not married. That's why her aunt has to adopt . . ."

"I'm not listening," said Jonathan, and he pretended to snore. But he didn't go to sleep. When sleep finally came, it was like a dark cloud settling over him.

The next thing he knew, Dad was calling him. There were sounds of much talk in the house again. Robert was up already. Jonathan felt bad about having yelled at him. He'd tell Robert he wouldn't be leaving for a long time. He'd be his friend forever. He stretched and stumbled his way to the living room.

Robert's mother had returned. Robert sat on the couch next to his little sisters. The girls were showing off their painted fingernails and toenails. They asked, "Will our next sitter paint our nails like Janice does?"

"We'll see. We'll see, dears," said their mother. She was looking right at Jonathan. She seemed excited.

Everyone seemed excited, Mother and Dad the most. Jonathan could tell that, even though no one said a word. He looked around. The girls were sitting on their hands now and holding their lips tightly shut.

Mother grabbed Jonathan and hugged him.

Dad roughed up his hair and said, "We've got a question to ask you, son."

Mother said, "You don't know what you started by bringing those storks to nest here, sweetheart."

Robert's mom said, "Robert, girls, I believe it is time we leave. This is a private family talk. I have to get you out of your pajamas. Sandra, you seemed the perfect one, especially after what Jonathan said. I do hope . . . but I'll understand."

"We got him! I can tell! Well, where is my baby brother?"

The girls began talking. Their mom shushed them and pulled them toward the door.

Mother said, "No. Don't leave. Let's just make sure Jonathan wants . . ." She paused. Then she began, like in his old birth story, "You were a wanted child, you know that, Jonathan."

Dad said, "We were happy just to have you and . . . We saw how well you made friends. We knew you'd never be lonely for playmates. So . . ."

Then Mother grabbed Robert and hugged him. "Thanks, Robert, for being such a friend to Jonathan."

"Well, where is the baby?" Jonathan wanted to know.

Everyone in the room held up two fingers.

"Twins?" Jonathan shouted.

Robert's mother said, "Twins. A boy and a girl. And Janice wants your family to adopt them."

"You didn't give them to the aunt?" Jonathan asked.

Robert's mother explained. "Janice knew she couldn't care for a baby and she wanted the best for it. Her aunt did agree to adopt it. But I'm afraid Janice failed to write one important detail. Maybe she feared her aunt would say no to twins. That is exactly what happened. Not all people can afford to adopt twins. Janice doesn't want them separated. So I came to ask your parents . . ."

Jonathan's eyes grew big. He charged Robert and slapped him a high five. "Look what the storks brought this time!"

"Jackpot!" yelled back Robert.

Then there was lots of hugging and laughing and some fast changing from pajamas to day clothes. Then they were off to the hospital to see two tiny babies.

"Twins sometimes are quite small," Mother explained, and handed both boys masks and gowns. When they were ready and seated, she handed each a baby.

Jonathan's tiny brother's head fit neatly into his hand.

"Who do they favor?" Robert asked.

"I don't know," said Jonathan. They looked awfully red. "I'd say my little sister has light hair like Mother, and me." His own face felt red-hot just saying that.

Mother laughed and said, "Your little brother's hair is dark like your father's. Well, like your father's when we were first married."

It made Jonathan think for a while. These babies were not his blood brother and sister. Mother had explained on the way to the hospital about this being an open adoption. Janice would receive pictures and keep in touch over the years.

"I think the boy has dark hair like Robert's," Jonathan said, and kindly traded babies with Robert.

Robert blushed. He liked that a lot.

"Well, okay, our little boy has hair like Robert's," said Mother. "They say everybody favors someone in this world."

Jonathan didn't mind that the baby looked like Robert. The babies were his, just like the storks were his, because he cared for them and loved them and had a part in naming them. He wanted the boy to have the name Greg, like his grandpa, Dad's father. Mother wanted the girl named Charlotte, for her mother. Jonathan okayed Mother's choice, so that counted, too.

Mother and Dad were standing. They looked happy, studying little Greg and Charlotte.

It felt good being an older brother. He guessed this was a good time to ask a question he had been wanting to ask. "Can I sleep over at Robert's tonight?"

His mother and father both were saying, "Oh, Jonathan, we weren't ignoring you. You are our firstborn. We want you with us."

"I know," Jonathan said. He didn't say how eager he was to try Robert's different toys and games. Robert also had a secret drawer in his chest. It was locked and Robert had the only key. That was so his sisters couldn't open it. Robert had told about it in a school report once.

Jonathan guessed he'd better check on this lock business. Twins would be getting into everything. Being an older brother could be really challenging. Wait until he reported these twins at school.

Jonathan shook his head to clear his thoughts.

Sally would say the storks didn't bring these babies. She'd say the storks were in Africa.

He didn't let it bother him, once he was at Robert's and playing hard, but about midnight he began thinking about it again. Midnight was when he and Robert went to bed, played out.

He guessed stork-luck came in lots of different ways. He and Robert had become friends because of the storks, right? Robert's mom and Mother had become friends because of the storks, right? Janice had come to watch the day the first stork arrived, right? So what if things didn't happen on a set day? Who's counting?

Sally, that's who. Finally, Jonathan giggled, relieved.

"What's so funny?" asked Robert.

"A baby takes nine months! I was just counting wrong, as long as it took stork eggs to hatch. I just hadn't figured the time it takes for people babies to be born. But the magic was there—Janice did show up on the day the male stork arrived, which meant she was to be part of the magic when it came. You know, I think magic comes in its time."

"Yeah. Sure," said Robert. "Go to sleep."

Jonathan did go to sleep, happy, and a little sad. He'd figured things out too well. He had sort of liked being the only boy the storks had brought.

Bringing the babies home helped lift the sad

part a bit. They were so cute! Robert kept talking about how the boy twin looked like him. He always insisted on holding Greg. Jonathan didn't mind. He liked the way his tiny sister's head fit into his hand and how her eyes looked right at him. It would be all right to share the luck with these twin babies.

Anyway, all was gladness by the spring when Adam and Ann nested again on the old brick wall. Victor and Violet took mates and stayed, as well. The clattering of stork bills and the feeling of good luck again filled the air.

The news people took pictures of the storks and of Jonathan and Robert. Robert said, "Notice how the headline reads, 'The Boys Who Brought the Storks Back.' It's not like the one in your old clipping that said, 'The Boy the Storks Brought.'"

"Well, things have changed as I've gotten older. But it's a good change," Jonathan said. "I was ready for broader horizons. You know that, Robert?"

"Whatever that means," answered Robert.

But Jonathan knew. He really did, though he couldn't put it into words. He just looked to the sky and the soaring storks. He was glad he'd returned to his birthplace and got a touch of magic once more. It was important for him to find it.

ABOUT THE AUTHOR

B erniece Rabe grew up in Missouri during the Depression, in a home with ten brothers and sisters, seven stepbrothers and stepsisters, and one half sister.

Her imaginative powers were developed during those hard times, and since childhood she has been fascinated by storks—for their beauty and grace, but also because they are said to bring good luck.

Berniece Rabe has published articles, award-winning short stories, and fifteen children's books. She was won the National Children's Choice Award and two Golden Kite awards. Five of her books have appeared on the National Social Studies List, and two have been listed by *School Library Journal* as Best of the Decade.

She speaks often, throughout the United States and in other countries. She lives with her husband in Sleepy Hollow, Illinois.

ABOUT THE ILLUSTRATOR

Doron Ben-Ami was drawing from the moment he was able to hold a crayon. "I love what I do," he says. "I want the characters in my illustrations to convey emotion in an absolutely convincing way."

Doron Ben-Ami was born in Tel-Aviv, Israel, and was graduated from Brooklyn College. He lives in Newtown, Connecticut, with his wife and two children.